Ballywhinney Girl

Eve Bunting

ILLUSTRATED BY

Emily Arnold McCully

CLARION BOOKS

Houghton Mifflin Harcourt

Boston   New York   2012

Clarion Books
215 Park Avenue South
New York, New York 10003

Clarion Books is an imprint of Houghton Mifflin Harcourt Publishing Company.

www.hmhbooks.com

The illustrations in this book were done in watercolor and pen and ink.
The text was set in Pastonchi MT Std.
Hand-lettering by Leah Palmer Preiss

Library of Congress Cataloging-in-Publication Data is available.
ISBN 978-0-547-55843-1

Manufactured in China
LEO 10 9 8 7 6 5 4 3 2 1
4500333861

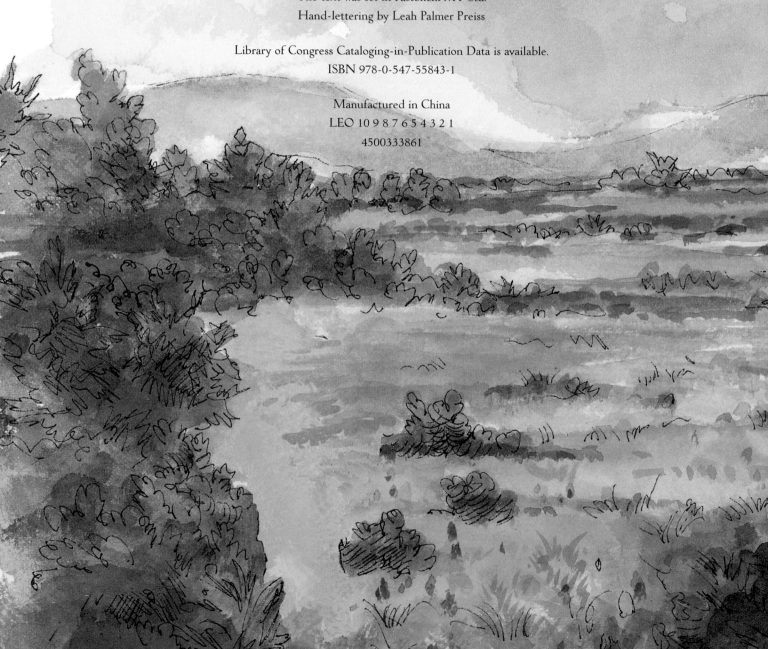

For Glenn Davison Bunting
—E.B.

We found her in the bog,
where she had lain so long.

It was my grandpa, cutting turf
for our kitchen fire, who found her.

His spade lifted peat dirt
from her face.
He staggered back.
"Arragh!" he whispered.
"Maeve! I've found a dead boy
buried in the bog.
Murdered maybe,
hidden here.
I'm stupefied, I am!
Run on home and
tell your ma.
Tell her to phone
the Ballywhinney police.
Go on now! Hurry, girl!"

I ran.
My ma,
eyes wide and staring,
called the town police.
"Stay here now, Maeve.
Don't you be going back," she said.

But I raced
back to the waiting bog.
She didn't see me leave,
for she was phoning
my Aunt Bridget and my da
and all the neighbors
to tell them
what had happened.

I crouched beside
my grandpa,
looking at this
outlandish thing.
A small black body,
buried in our bog!

The Ballywhinney police
came in their car.
"Jakers! Will you look at that!"
they said.
"You've found a mummy,
all of him preserved
in peat for centuries."
The sergeant scratched his head
beneath his cap.
"We'll get the word to Dublin
and they'll send
a team of archaeologists.
Don't go near him
till they come."

They came, the archaeologists,
excited and aware
of the importance of our find.

My grandpa,
cold and shaking,
held my hand.

"You should go home,"
the sergeant said to me.
I acted like I didn't hear,
and stayed.

I wasn't sure exactly how I felt.
There was fear
and curiosity,
but there was more.
Something I could not
put a name to.

My grandpa said,
"You're tellin' me
this boy's been buried here
and lay a hundred years or so
before we found him?
It's bewildering, so it is."

"A hundred years?"
an archaeologist replied.
"I'd guess a thousand.
Maybe more."

My grandpa gasped.
"You hear that, Maeve?
A thousand years,
and him in there!"

So long ago! It dazed my mind.
A thousand years would be
before the motorcars or telephones
or even television.
I shook my head, confused.
"You'd almost think
that yesterday he was alive
and walking, just like you or me.
You would, except his skin.
He's got a suntan
that he never got in Ballywhinney!"

Another archaeologist bent close
to where the mummy lay.
"He might not even be a he.
I'm thinking he's a she."

I gasped.
A girl!
A girl like me, a thousand years ago
dead and dropped into this quiet place.
Who was she?
What had happened?
My heart was beating awful fast.
I wished I knew.

My grandpa looked at me,
then took my hand.
"Don't you go fretting, Maeve.
I think she was a miracle, this girl,
just waiting to be found."

The archaeologist agreed.
"The chances are
she lived in this townland,
died, and was buried in the bog.
Or else she fell and sank,
never to be found—
till now.
The bog turns light skin dark,
like leather,
but lifelike just the same."

My grandpa shook his head.
"It's more than I can comprehend.
A mystery, is what it is."

The neighbors all had come,
alerted by my ma.
My da was on his way, she said.
He works in Lisnaglen.

The police held the people back.
Me and my grandpa were
allowed to stay,
as well we should be.
We had found her.

The men from Dublin
placed our mummy in a box,
moving her with care
because her bones
were thin as glass.
That's what they told us.
They packed fat wadding round her
so she could not slide and break.

"Where are you taking her?" I asked.

"We'll take her to the lab
in Dublin, where they'll do some tests:
X-rays and scans.
They'll let us know."

It made me sad to see her go.
I touched the box
they'd placed her in,
and rubbed the wood.
I didn't like to think of her inside,
so closed and dark,
so like the coffin
that she'd never had.

"You'll keep her safe?" I asked,
and heard my voice
all scratchy-sore.
"And don't forget,
we were the ones who found her.
In a way, she's ours."

"You'll tell us all they find?"
my grandpa asked.

"You'll be the first to know,"
they said.

A week passed by.
And then
the sergeant came.
He had a cup of tea
and ate a slice of soda bread
with jam,
like he was one of us.

"They did the tests," he said.

I wondered if they'd hurt, those tests.
Had they stuck needles in her?
Cut her open? What?
Sometimes I wished
that we had never found her.

"There was some hair
still clinging to her head.
Fair, like yours, young Maeve,
and there were scraps of leggings
round her legs, and some torn rags
that might have been a cloak
that someone sewed from animal skins."

I pictured her, so long ago,
dressing herself and putting on the cloak
her mother made.
Was she on her way to school?
And did she take a shortcut
through the bog?
Would there be schools
away back then?

"They found some flowers beside her,"
the sergeant said.
He took another sip of tea.
"Stalks like sticks, and petals
see-through clear.
They think that they were lupin
and wild roses,
the kind that line the lanes
of Ballywhinney."

I saw her dawdling along the lanes
the way I do.
I heard her singing as she walked.

The sergeant said that newsmen came,
a host of them,
but they were told to stay away.
Their camera flashes could destroy the find.

I interrupted him. *"Our* find!"
"That's true. Your find," he said.

But we could tell that
there were those who hunted news,
whose cameras took pictures
as she lay,
their lenses zooming in
to almost touch
the dark, dead face
that filled our television screens
night after night.
I closed my eyes.

The *Ballywhinney Gazette* said
they had named her.
"She'll be Ballywhinney Girl
for Ballywhinney,
where she was found," they wrote.
"They're going to freeze-dry her
so she won't decay
and put her on display
in Dublin, in the museum
where other mummies lie."

"Do you think she's glad
to be set free from where she was?"
I asked my da, who knows a lot.

"She's dead, me darlin', dead and gone.
The dead don't know or care."

I wonder, though.

I wonder, did she like
her sweet, warm resting place?
And did she like it more
than that cold viewing case
where she will lie
from now until forever?

I begged my da to take me
into Dublin
so that I could see her
one last time.
My ma and grandpa came along.

She lay curled up,
her body black as coal
and full of secrets.
So pitiful to see
those tufts of hair
as blond as mine.
It made me cry.

When we got home
I found a big, flat rock
and set it on the place
where once she'd lain.

I said goodbye.

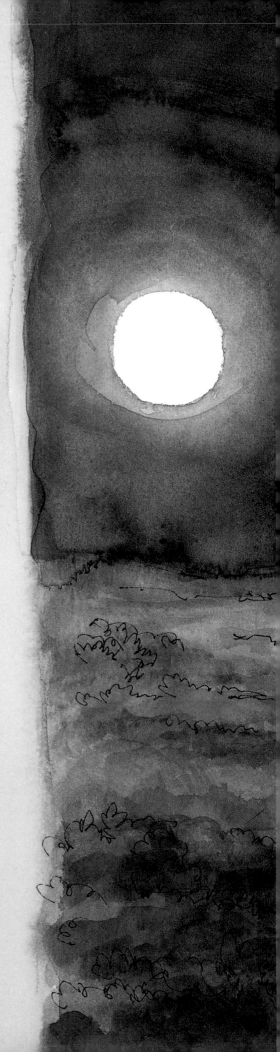

Out on the bog
the wind blows soft
across the closed-in hole
across the stone
that marks her place.
And on a moonlit night
you still may see her there,
walking on the bog she loved.

She carries flowers,
blue lupin and wild roses.
Her ghost-light steps
are gentle on the place
where long ago she fell.

Stay quiet now!
And do not speak
or she may vanish.

Afterword

A bog is a stretch of wet, spongy land found in places that have heavy rainfall, such as Ireland. Plants and grasses grow on its surface. There are mosses in the acidic soil. Partly decayed trees and plants mash together in the bog to make peat. The mosses and peat contain natural preservatives, so anything that sinks in the bog decays very slowly.

Irish villagers often go out onto the bog and cut bricklike blocks of peat to burn in their fireplaces. There is nothing that smells as sweet or burns as richly as a peat fire. These diggings into the bogs sometimes turn up primitive weapons and tools. The diggers have also unearthed ancient bones and even mummified human bodies, like the fictional Ballywhinney Girl. More than eighty such mummies have been found in Irish bogs. Many more have been unearthed in other countries with similar weather and soil conditions. One of the earliest mummies discovered was the Koelbjerg Woman, found in Denmark. Archaeologists dated her body back to about 8000 BC.

Some mummified bodies have been handled with reverence and respect when found. Others were treated as curiosities to be exhibited in freak shows or offered at auction. Still others were ground up into "mummy powder" and sold for medicinal use.

New machinery used by commercial peat cutters can destroy mummies before they are ever found. But others may lie hidden in their deep, dark graves forever. Bogs have been mysteries for thousands of years and do not easily give up their secrets.